Bess the Book Bus

Written by Concetta M. Payne and Freda Roberts
Illustrated by Andrieanna Barnes

ISBN 978-1-936352-62-3
1-936352-62-1

Published by Mirror Publishing
Milwaukee, WI 53214

Printed at Worzalla Publishing in Stevens Point, WI. U.S.A.
072011

We sincerely thank Jennifer Frances, the creator and owner of Bess the Book Bus Inc., for her authorization to use the title and logo for our book "Bess the Book Bus".

Thank you to the Ford Motor Company for the privilege of being able to use a picture of the Ford Transit Connect along with the Ford Emblem, and for having presented the vehicle to Jennifer.

Everyone calls me "Bess the Book Bus", but I am NOT A PASSENGER BUS! I am a VERY SPECIAL BUS.

I would like to tell you how I got my name. My owner and dear friend Jennifer Frances named me in memory of her nana, Bess O'Keefe. Bess was nicknamed "Nana Bus". She taught Jennifer the importance and joy of reading.

Jennifer's dream is to deliver free books to all the children that don't have access to them. That is why I'm a VERY... VERY... SPECIAL BUS! Without Jennifer's help I could not be making this journey.

I am a bright yellow bus with my name painted in thick black letters along each side. When you climb on board "Bess the Book Bus" you will find stacks and stacks of children's books waiting to be given to as many children as possible.

Little did I know what my journey would be like?
There were times when I got totally exhausted,
like the time I was huffing and puffing trying to
get up this huge hill. When I finally made it to the
top I shouted, "YIPPIE I MADE IT!"

Some days it rained so hard I became completely soaked! Those were the days when I really needed an umbrella, but that was a silly thought. I knew perfectly well there wasn't an umbrella big enough to cover me. Come rain or come shine I was determined to keep on rolling.

I had about two miles to go to reach my next destination. As I pulled into this large parking lot I saw many signs that read "WELCOME BESS THE BOOK BUS!"

Before you knew it there were people coming from everywhere. They were all rushing to see me, and to come on board. One by one they boarded "Bess the Book Bus". Every child left with a free book and a smile on their face.

I was just about to call it a day when a little boy approached me. He was a handsome little guy, and told me is name was Tommy. He had asked me whether I had any horse books because they were his favorite animal. I had told him to go on board and look around.

A short time later I noticed Tommy was carrying a book. He came up to me and said, "I found a really cool horse book. Thank you so much Bess. Is it really mine to keep?" With a broad smile on my face I said, "It sure is Tommy".

Tommy walked closer reached up and kissed my cheek. That was certainly a beautiful way to end a long day.

When I awoke the next morning all I could think about were the many miles I had to travel to my next stop. I went over my list making sure everything was a go. My gas tank was full and the oil had been checked. There were plenty of books to be given out, so I started my engine and headed out.

I decided to turn on some music as I concentrated on the roadway. ALL OF A SUDDEN I HEARD A BIG POPPING SOUND! Oh no, I hope it isn't what I think it is.

I pulled over to the side of the road, looked out the window and saw my tire was completely flat! I shouted, WHAT AM I GOING TO DO?

I WILL NOT DISAPPOINT THE CHILDREN! There wasn't a single car in sight, and I knew being stranded was going to cause a major problem. I sat and waited, hoping that someone would come along to help me.

It seemed like hours, but as I looked in my rear view mirror a car had pulled up behind me. A gentleman got out of his car and walked over to me. He told me his name was James, and he asked me if I needed help.

I quickly answered yes, and thanked him for stopping. I told him where the spare tire was located, and he got right to work.

While James was changing the tire I also told him all about my reasons for being there. During our conversation, James had mentioned he had two children and how much they love books. It didn't take long before James told me I was ready to move on. As a token of my appreciation, I asked James to please pick out a book for each of his children.

I was finally rolling again, and I was so grateful that James had helped me. After a few miles, I started looking for the exit sign that read Main

When I turned onto Main Street I saw crowds of people lined up on both sides of the street. There were balloons, clowns, refreshment stands, flags waving and very loud music coming from all the speakers. They were all shouting, "HERE COMES BESS THE BOOK BUS - HI BESS THE

The excitement that I felt was overwhelming! There were lines of children all eager to get on board. Everyone politely waited their turn. You could tell from their smiles that they didn't mind the wait.

Even though I had gotten a flat tire, that day turned out to be a SUPER HAPPY ONE!   That evening I checked my supply of books, then got ready for a good night's sleep.

The next morning I headed back to my hometown of Tampa, Florida. My friend Jennifer received many books that were donated by generous supporters of "Bess the Book Bus". She restacked my supply of books, and had a list of all the places

From there I will continue my journey delivering free books to as many children as I can reach. Thank you for enabling me to delight children and to "Explore the World Cover to Cover".